Sharon,

Thank you for all of you[illegible]
this year. I thought this book had a
special message. I hope you enjoy
it.

Best Wishes this Holiday season!

[illegible] Brose

To Ned.
Your spirit is in every brush stroke
and in every line.
TH & WH

Hegg, Tom.
A memory of Christmas tea / Tom Hegg : illustrated by Warren Hanson.
p. cm.
Sequel to: A cup of Christmas tea.
Summary: On a lonely Christmas a nephew remembers his beloved great aunt and realizes the value of her legacy, a message of advice revealing the true spirit of the season.
ISBN 0-931674-39-5 (alk. paper)
[1. Christmas--Fiction. 2. Great-aunts--Fiction. 3. Stories in rhyme.] I. Hanson, Warren, ill. II. Title.
PZ8.3.H398Me 1999
[Fic]--dc21 99-12669

Waldman House Press, Inc.
525 North Third Street
Minneapolis, Minnesota 55401

ISBN: 0-931674-39-5
Printed in the United States of America
Third Printing

by Tom Hegg
illustrated by Warren Hanson

Waldman House Press

The Christmas list was growing
as my time was running out.

Chicago!!
CALL MOM
Send B.N.
2:00
pick up

I seemed to meet myself
in stores and malls. I rushed about.
I felt that life was going
at an ever-faster clip —
And, zip! Another shopping day
had given me the slip.

With empty hands, I headed home,
a pile of work in store.
I fumbled with my keys
beneath the wreath upon the door.

I looked around. The tree was trimmed.
The stockings were in place.
The stage was set, and yet I didn't
feel the slightest trace
Of Christmas in the air.
It might as well have been July.
The pieces didn't fit together,
and I wondered why.

I opened up the mail...
turned the TV on and off...
I listened to my messages
and thought about my cough.

December afternoons are quick
to darken into night.
I stumbled to the kitchen
and I flicked the switch. The light
Was blinding for a moment,
so I had to shut my eyes.
And when I opened them again,
they fell, to my surprise,
Upon a sight that I had seen
so many times before —
So often that I hardly even saw it
anymore —

My Great Aunt's Christmas china.
I had put it on display
Exactly as I had for years,
upon the very day
That all the boxes from the attic
always come downstairs.
How odd that something so well-known
should catch me unawares.

She'd left the service and
her cherished ornaments to me,
Requesting, as her legacy,
a cup of Christmas tea
That I would share with someone else,
as we had always done —
My Christmas promise —
that I had not kept with anyone.

I felt a twinge of guilt for that.
Excuses leapt to mind.
Both time and opportunities
were things I couldn't find.

My life was an emergency, a crisis,
and a race
With problems running after me
and at me at a pace
That only was accelerating
as the years flew by.
So if I couldn't stop for tea,
I had my reasons why.

And then, I heard my parents —
in my mind, but loud and clear —
Reminding us to mind our manners.
"This is once a year,
So please be careful
at your Great Aunt's house."
And we would leave,
All scrubbed within an inch of our
young lives, for Christmas Eve.

A host of cousins, aunts and uncles
would be coming, too.
Oh, it was so exciting,
it was all that I could do
To keep myself from flying!
Then we took that final right
And pulled up to the wooden house.
Activity and light
Were dancing in the windows,
and the laughter of the crowd
Came floating out upon
a sugar-cookie-scented cloud.

"Come in! Come in!" She laughed the words.
She took me by the hand,
And Christmas Eve began again,
as if by her command.

The years went by... and phrases such as
"My, how you have grown!"
Became "She really shouldn't try
to do all this alone."
Yet on and on she went —
the last to sit, the first to rise —
My Great Aunt with her family
in dresses, coats and ties.

Then came her final dinner
by the fragrant balsam fir.
But Father Time, who claims us all,
had quite a time with her.
Though delicate and fragile
as a fine bone china cup,
No matter how he troubled her,
she kept on looking up.

And when, at last, she brewed
her final cup of Christmas tea,
She didn't do it for herself.
I know it was for me.
I saw her look me in the eye
and ask of me, "What's new?"
And I remember telling her
of all I meant to do.

I know that she believed me —
and believed in me — in spite
Of times that I had failed her...
as I nearly had that night.
I'd taken her for granted,
as I grew into my prime,
And now, my old Great Aunt
had lost the luxury of time.

I didn't know that this would be
our final cup of tea.
I only knew that my Great Aunt
was listening to me.
She listened, so that I would never
choose to waste my days
By going through the motions
in a dim, unfeeling haze.
She listened, spending down her last
reserves of inner strength,
That I might never settle
for self-pitying at length,

Or hide behind my busyness,
or use my hurts and fears
To justify the compromise of conscience
through the years,
Or ever be so ugly as to judge
another soul,
To put my greed and selfishness
ahead of self-control,
Or dwell upon the negative,
or wait for life to prove
That everything would go my way
before I dared to move.

Merry Chris
mas

She didn't wish me money,
and she didn't wish me fame.
She didn't care if throngs of people
ever knew my name.
She gave her final prayer
that I might finally arrive,
In faith that I could make it,
find the truth, and come alive.
I'd look into another's eyes.
I'd trust and really see.
I'd do for just one person
what my Great Aunt did for me.

I thought I heard a car pull up,
and then I checked the clock.
I had to start my pile of work...
and then, there came a knock.

The door was double-locked.
I clicked the latch and slid the bolt…
The wood was swollen,
but I popped it open with a jolt.
A rush of crystal air…
a silhouette against the sky…
A hush… a pair of eyes met mine…
a gentle voice said, "Hi."
"Come in! Come in!" I laughed the words.
I took a hand in mine —

And then, it felt like Christmas...
and the lights began to shine,
The bells began to ring again,
and spices filled the air,

And all I knew of time
was that the time was ours to share.

I took two cups. I smiled...
and when I saw a smile for me,
We settled back together
for a cup of Christmas tea.